RACIAL JUSTICE IN AMERICA

AAPI EXCELLENCE AND ACHIEVEMENT

EXCELLENCE in STEM

VIRGINIA LOH-HAGAN

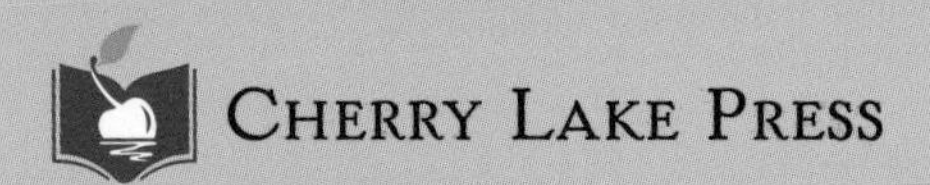

Published in the United States of America by Cherry Lake Publishing Group
Ann Arbor, Michigan
www.cherrylakepublishing.com

Reading Adviser: Beth Walker Gambro, MS, Ed., Reading Consultant, Yorkville, IL
Book Design and Cover Art: Felicia Macheske

Photo Credits: © Monkey Business Images/Shutterstock, 5; Smithsonian Institution Archives via Flickr, 7; © tilialucida/Shutterstock, 9; NASA, 10; © aprilante/Shutterstock, 13; © Suzanne Tucker/Shutterstock, 14; © AngieYeoh/Shutterstock, 16; Library of Congress, Photo by Alfred A. Hart, LOC Control No: 2005683011, 19; Via Wikimedia (Public Domain) Source: http://www.wulunpaimai.com/news_show.aspx?id=202, 19; © Theerayoot/Shutterstock, 21; © RichLegg/iStock, 23; Stefan Zachow of the International Mathematical Union via Wikimedia (Public Domain), 25; © RomanR/Shutterstock, 25; © Naeblys/Shutterstock, 27; © dpa picture alliance/Alamy Stock Photo, 28; © RonTech3000/Shutterstock, 30

Graphics Throughout: © debra hughes/Shutterstock; © Galyna_P/Shutterstock

Cherry Lake Press is an imprint of Cherry Lake Publishing Group.

Library of Congress Cataloging-in-Publication Data has been filed and is available at catalog.loc.gov.

Cherry Lake Publishing Group would like to acknowledge the work of the Partnership for 21st Century Learning, a Network of Battelle for Kids. Please visit *http://www.battelleforkids.org/networks/p21* for more information.

Printed in the United States of America
Corporate Graphics

Dr. Virginia Loh-Hagan is an author, former K-8 teacher, curriculum designer, and university professor. She's currently the director of the Asian Pacific Islander Desi American (APIDA) Center at San Diego State University. She is also the co-executive director of the Asian American Education Project. She identifies as Chinese American and is committed to amplifying APIDA communities.

CHAPTER 1

AAPI in STEM

Asian Americans and Pacific Islanders (AAPI) are part of the American story. They have made and continue to make significant contributions. But they've also been mistreated. In response to this, they stand in solidarity as a united front to fight for racial justice. But it's important to remember that AAPI communities have unique cultures, histories, and languages.

AAPI have excelled in STEM. *STEM* stands for Science, Technology, Engineering, and Math. But achieving excellence has not been easy. The community has faced many barriers. They have been denied education and jobs. They have not been given credit for their work.

Another big issue with STEM is that not all AAPI are treated equally. Many Chinese Americans and Indian Americans work in STEM industries. This is great, but more representation for other groups is also important. More Southeast Asians and Pacific Islanders should be involved in STEM.

AAPI followed their passions and dreams. They overcame obstacles. AAPI in STEM have improved the lives of others. They have solved all kinds of problems. This book aims to acknowledge their contributions.

STEAM is another acronym. It adds "arts" to STEM.

CHAPTER 2

Excellence in Science

Many AAPI have found success as scientists. Scientists dedicate their lives to research. They find answers to questions about the world.

A notable Asian American scientist is Dr. Chien-Shiung Wu. She's called the "first lady of physics." She moved from China to the United States to earn a **doctorate** in physics. Wu was hired to work on the Manhattan Project. This top secret project led to the creation of the atomic bomb. In 1956, Wu led an experiment known as the Wu experiment. This experiment helped two men, Dr. Tsung-Dao Lee and Dr. Chen-Ning Yang, win the Nobel Prize in 1957.

Wu's work and research experience advanced physics. Many thought she should have won the Nobel Prize as well. While she never received a Nobel Prize, Wu received many other honors. She was the first woman to teach at Princeton University in New Jersey. She was also the first female president of the American Physical Society. In this role, she met U.S. President Gerald Ford. She convinced him to form an advisory science board. She overcame **sexism** and anti-Asian feelings. She leaves a lasting legacy and continues to be a role model for women in science.

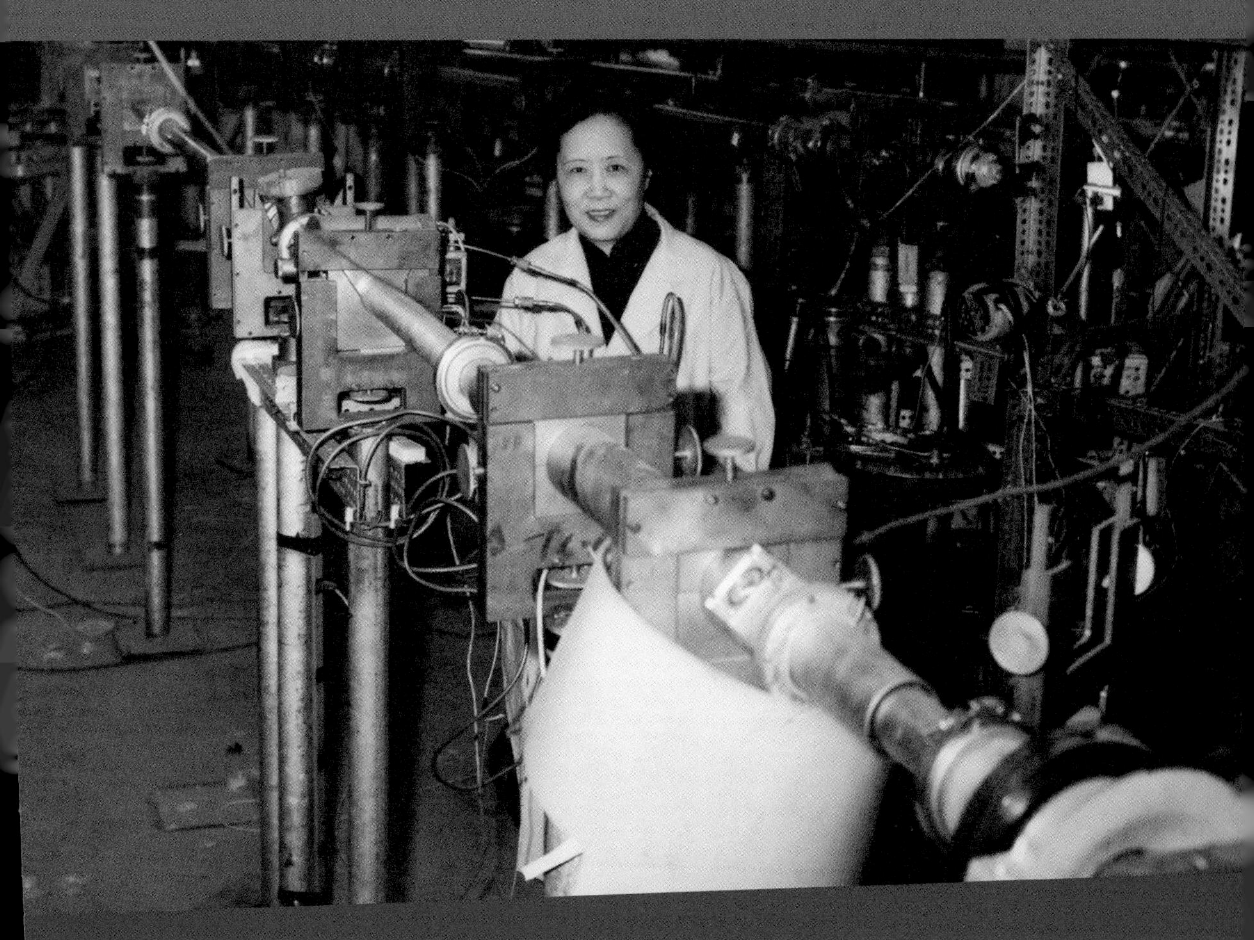

Many women scientists, like Dr. Chien-Shiung Wu, are paid less than their male coworkers. Wu fought for equal pay and inspired other women to do so as well.

Dr. Isabella Aiona Abbott is another female role model. She was the first Native Hawaiian woman to get a doctorate in science. As a woman, she had a hard time finding jobs. She eventually became the first woman and first non-White biology professor at Stanford University. She researched seaweed. She discovered more than 200 seaweed species. She valued native knowledge. She wanted people to be mindful about eating and using plants. She created recipes using seaweed.

FUN FACT!

Before reading this book, how many AAPI scientists could you name? If your list was small, you're not alone. A national study found that about half of Americans couldn't name a notable AAPI person in any field. AAPI are rarely mentioned in science textbooks. A 2020 study examined biology textbooks used in U.S. colleges. Fewer than 3 percent of scientists mentioned were of Asian descent. There was no mention of Pacific Islanders. More than 85 percent of the scientists included were White males. Representation matters. Women and people of color need to see themselves in STEM fields. More diversity in STEM textbooks will increase interest in STEM fields.

Many scientists work as professors at universities. Universities provide lab spaces where scientists do their research.

Medical scientists keep us healthy. In 2020, the world suffered from the COVID-19 **pandemic**. But by 2021, vaccines were available. Thanks can be given to Dr. Flossie Wong-Staal. Wong-Staal was a Chinese American scientist. She studied diseases, including the **HIV** virus. She was the first to **clone** the virus. She figured out how it invaded the body. Her work helped fight **AIDS**. It also led to the development of the COVID-19 vaccines. But there is little public mention of her work. In 2008, she was passed over for a Nobel Prize. She also faced racial discrimination. Born in China, her birth name was Wong Yee Ching. She changed her name to fit in. Her father suggested "Flossie" after a typhoon that hit Southeast Asia. She died in 2020 at the age of 73.

Dr. Ted Fujita was a Japanese American **meteorologist** who studied typhoons and other storms. He was known as "Mr. Tornado." He gathered data from hundreds of tornado sites. He developed the Fujita Scale, which measures the strength of tornadoes. His work helped people understand severe weather. Pilot training programs use his research to better prepare students for flying in severe storms. Like Wong-Staal, his work has saved lives as it has led to more robust pilot trainings and aviation warning systems.

About 8 percent of NASA's employees are Asian American or Pacific Islander. They perform all types of work. Only a small number of employees go to space. Pictured is Ellison S. Onizuka.

AAPI scientists are also advancing space science. In 1985, Ellison S. Onizuka became the first Asian American astronaut to fly in space. Sadly, he died in 1987 during his second mission when his shuttle exploded during liftoff. He helped advance space travel.

Dr. Roseli Ocampo-Friedmann's work took us even farther. A Filipina American scientist, she studied **microorganisms**. She showed that microscopic life could exist on Mars. She traveled all over the world. She went to extreme environments like Antarctica. She collected more than 1,000 types of microorganisms.

Indian American **aerospace** scientist Dr. Swati Mohan is exploring life on Mars. She was part of the National Aeronautics and Space Administration's (NASA) Mars 2020 mission.

CHAPTER 3

Excellence in Technology

Technology includes devices, the internet, and much more. It changes with the times. AAPI have excelled in the technology field. Their inventions have helped create our digital world. Technology has improved communications. Can you imagine your life without technology?

The COVID-19 pandemic impacted everyone. The world isolated to stop the spread. But we were still able to connect with family and friends. Even in isolation, school and work continued. This was in great part thanks to Chinese American Eric Yuan. Yuan started the company Zoom Video Communications.

Yuan was born in China. He was always interested in technology. He knew that to succeed he had to move to the United States because of its tech boom. But getting to the United States proved difficult. He had to apply for immigration nine times. Once in the United States, Yuan was treated unfairly. He didn't speak English well, so he wasn't taken seriously. But he persisted. He created a smartphone-friendly video conferencing system inspired by his college experience. While attending college in China, he often visited his girlfriend. He had to travel by train for 10 hours. He thought there must be an easier way to see her, and he created it. But the company he worked for rejected his idea. So Yuan started his own company, Zoom. He recalled advice from his father: "Keep working hard. Stay humble. And someday you'll be OK."

Technology continues to advance with time. Thousands of years ago, the wheel was considered advanced technology!

High-speed internet is needed for optimal online gaming. Today, more Asian Americans work as game developers. More Asian Americans means better representation in the games.

Computer technology is constantly improving. Years ago, only experts could use computers. Ajay Bhatt is an Indian American computer scientist. He helped make tech easy for everyone to use. He created several widely used tech tools. He's most famous for inventing the Universal Series Bus (USB). Before Bhatt, connecting keyboards, mouses, and printers to a computer was hard. It also took a lot of time. Only users with tech skills could do it. Bhatt's USB made it easy to connect different devices to computers. The USB serves as a translator. It helps computers understand different commands.

Other important AAPI inventors benefited technology. Dr. Narinder Singh Kapany was an example. He was an Indian American physicist. He's called the "father of fiber optics." Fiber optics is a way of sending data through thin threads called fibers. The data travels through the fibers as light. Fiber optic cables link televisions, computers, and telephones. Doctors use fiber optic tools to see inside the human body. Kapany was an expert on fiber optics. He wrote many articles and created many inventions. But his top achievement is laying the foundation for high-speed internet technology.

FUN FACT!

Tech jobs pay well. However, these jobs are dominated by men. Few women become computer programmers. Only about 20 percent of computer science majors are women. Reshma Saujani wants to change this. She founded Girls Who Code. This group teaches young girls to code. Vivian Phung attended a Girls Who Code program. She became inspired to code. In college, she used her coding skills. She learned her friend struggled with finding bathrooms that fit their gender identity. She worked with other coders. She created an app that helps users find gender-neutral bathrooms in the United States.

The internet has changed our lives. AAPI have led the way in the internet industry. Before Google, there was Yahoo. In 2000, it was the most popular website in the world. Yahoo was co-founded by Jerry Yang. Yang is a Taiwanese American computer programmer. He liked to program as a hobby. While studying at Stanford University, he created an internet website called "Jerry and David's Guide to the World Wide Web." This site eventually became Yahoo.

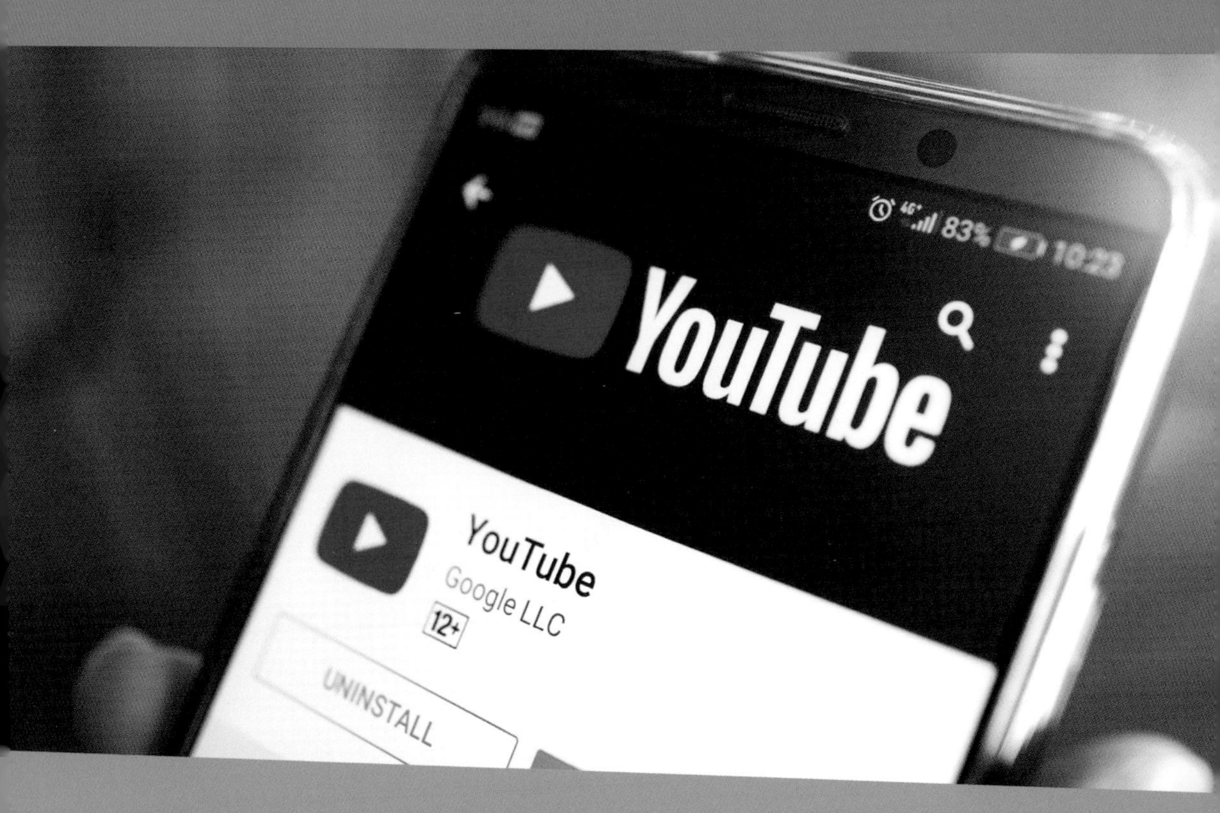

Wong Fu Productions is a filmmaking group. It is one of the original trailblazers of AAPI YouTubers.

Yahoo pioneered many internet concepts. It was the first popular search engine. It created the first web directory, an online list of websites. Yahoo introduced **cloud storage**. It was the first website to add various news feeds. It added email, shopping, maps, and other services. Yahoo also introduced video-sharing and streaming websites.

In 2005, Chad Hurley, Steve Chen, and Jawed Karim invented YouTube. Steve Chen is a Taiwanese American computer scientist. Jawed Karim is a Bangladeshi American software engineer. YouTube is a free online video sharing website. Users can upload, publish, and watch videos. YouTube has provided us with hours and hours of entertainment.

Because of AAPI in tech, information is at our fingertips. Technology has made our lives easier.

CHAPTER 4

Excellence in Engineering

Engineers design and maintain engines, machines, and structures. They're inventors and builders. AAPI have had a big part in building the United States.

AAPI have connected us through technology. They've been important in building the **information superhighway** which has connected the world to each other. In the 1860s, Chinese Americans played a huge role in building the Transcontinental Railroad. This railroad line connected the East and West Coasts. Railroad companies relied heavily on cheap Chinese labor. Thousands of Chinese workers lost their lives. Despite this, they received very little credit for their work. They were also mistreated. They were paid less than White workers. They had to buy their own food and sleep in tents. White workers slept in train cars and received company meals.

The Transcontinental Railroad was a major engineering feat. Building the railroad was a lot of work. To lay tracks, the land had to first be cleared. The route included many dangerous obstacles such as mountains and cliffs. Chinese workers had the most dangerous jobs. They **bored** tunnels through mountains. They used **explosives**. Sometimes they were lowered off cliffs to blast rock. Some Chinese workers had experience with explosives.

The "four great inventions of China" are the compass, gunpowder, paper, and printing.

Engineers design buildings, bridges, and more. AAPI have built many famous structures. I. M. Pei was a Chinese American architect. He designed the John F. Kennedy Presidential Library and the Rock and Roll Hall of Fame and Museum. His best-known building is the glass pyramid at the Louvre Museum in Paris, France. He uses bold, geometric designs. Although Pei is the best known, he is far from the only AAPI architect. Minoru Yamasaki designed the original World Trade Center in New York. Maya Lin designed the Vietnam Veterans Memorial in Washington, D.C.

Dr. Fazlur Rahman Khan was a Bangladeshi American. He was called the "Einstein of **structural engineering**." It's because of him that we have skyscrapers. He invented the tube system. Tall buildings are subject to winds and other impacts. To resist these impacts, buildings can be built like tubes. Khan was inspired by the bamboo growing in his Bangladeshi hometown. His most famous design was the Willis Tower in Chicago. It was the world's tallest building from 1973 to 1998.

Pei's glass pyramid sparked much criticism and was even called an "architectural joke" as cited in *The New York Times Magazine*. Many felt it was too modern for the centuries-old space.

FUN FACT!

Engineering does not have to be complicated. Inventing simple tools is part of engineering. For example, Chinese American Joyce Chen invented the stir-fry pan. Chinese dishes are usually made in woks, which are bowl-shaped pans. Chen found that woks didn't work well on American stoves. In China, stoves have a circular hole. Chen invented a pan with a flat bottom. She called it the Peking Wok. Chen helped popularize Chinese food in the United States. She opened restaurants, had a cooking show, and wrote cookbooks. She also designed cooking utensils.

Engineers invent all kinds of things, big and small. AAPI have invented other important things. For example, Dr. Peter Tsai invented the N95 **respirator** mask. Tsai is a Taiwanese American **material scientist**. Originally, his masks were for industrial use. Dust on construction sites and factories floats into the air. Workers breathe it in and get sick. Tsai's masks protect people. They trap the dust in the fibers. They're more effective than other masks. The masks also block viruses. This was a game-changer during COVID-19 pandemic. In 2020, Tsai, who had retired, went back to work. He studies ways to clean and reuse the masks. He wants to make them better.

Dr. Tuan Vo-Dinh is a Vietnamese American. He is a scientist and inventor. As a boy, he invented his own toys. He is an expert on the use of light. He invented several life-saving **optical** devices. He created a badge that detects exposure to toxins. An optical scanner reveals the toxins. Vo-Dinh created other devices that detect and diagnose diseases. They help patients avoid surgeries that remove body tissues for testing. Vo-Dinh has saved people's lives.

Many common things we use every day were invented or designed by Asian Americans.

CHAPTER 5

Excellence in Math

Mathematicians study numbers. They make predictions to help people make decisions. They often work on problems for a long time. Their calculations help solve various problems. AAPI have counted their way to success.

Dr. Terence Tao is Australian and American. His parents are from China and Hong Kong. He's described as the "greatest mathematician of our time." He's also been called the "Mozart of math." He's considered one of the world's smartest people.

Tao loved math from a young age. He learned math from playing games and solving puzzles. He also credits *Sesame Street* for teaching him the basics. At 5 years old, he was teaching math to other kids. He started high school at age 7. Tao completed college at 16 and earned his doctorate at 21. He was awarded the MacArthur Genius Grant. He's won many top awards in math, including the Fields Medal. He said, "I wanted to use mathematics to explore and understand as much of the world as I could."

The Fields Medal is the most prestigious math award. It's often described as the "Nobel Prize in mathematics."

Taiwanese American Dr. Fan Chung has had to overcome sexism in her field of mathematics. She was the first tenured female math professor at the University of Pennsylvania. She had many female mentors. They inspired her to continue her pioneering work as a woman in mathematics.

More Southeast Asian Americans need to be mentored into top math positions. Vietnamese American mathematician Dr. Pham Huu Tiep is paving the way. He's a math professor at Rutgers University in New Jersey. In 2018, he was invited to speak at the International Congress of Mathematics. This conference is like a "hall of fame" for mathematicians. Tiep was only the fifth person of Vietnamese descent to speak at this conference.

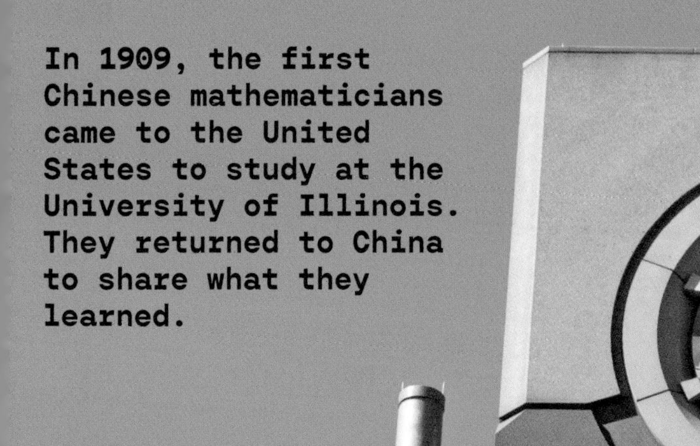

In 1909, the first Chinese mathematicians came to the United States to study at the University of Illinois. They returned to China to share what they learned.

The lives of sailors depend on good navigation. Navigation uses a lot of math. It requires measurements and calculations. Today, we use technology to navigate the seas. Early Pacific Islanders used traditional methods. They used the Sun, Moon, stars, clouds, and waves. Around the 14th century, they stopped using this knowledge. This was around the time compasses were popularized.

Nainoa Thompson is a Native Hawaiian navigator. He is the first modern Hawaiian to use native knowledge. In the 1980s, he traveled more than 16,000 nautical miles (29,632 kilometers) among the Pacific Islands in a canoe without using Western tools. Thompson invented the modern Hawaiian star compass. The compass is a visual form of how navigators view the horizon. Navigators find their location by identifying the position of the stars. They also use birds, waves, and other things from nature.

Some mathematicians found jobs where they can apply their math. Josephine Jue is a Chinese American mathematician. She uses her math skills to program computers. She is the first Asian American woman to work at NASA. When she started, she was one of only eight women and the only Asian American woman. She was the chief of NASA's Software Engineering Lab. She developed code for the space shuttle program.

The International Mathematical Olympiad (IMO) is a world championship contest for high school students. It's held in a different place each year.

Actuaries use math and **statistics**. They measure and manage risk. Sherry Chan served as New York City's chief actuary. She's the first woman and person of color to be in this role. She said, "I always had a passion for math . . . I wanted to use it in my career in a way that I could see its effects in the real world." She managed the city's budget and workers' **pensions**.

Roy Ju is a Chinese American. He's a fellow of the Society of Actuaries (SOA). This is SOA's top professional designation. At age 20, Ju was the youngest person to receive this honor. He had to take classes and pass a series of exams. He started taking the exams as a junior in high school.

Another job for mathematicians is teaching. Dr. Peter Esperanza is a Filipino American. He taught high school in Barstow, California. He created a YouTube channel for math teachers and students. He posts free online math videos. He also includes content in the Filipino language. He's now a math professor at Barstow Community College.

AAPI have and continue to make breakthroughs in STEM. They are helping solve the world's problems.

Ask your teacher about how you can learn more about AAPI in STEM.

ACHiEVE EXCELLENCE!

The future of AAPI excellence is you! If you identify as AAPI, make your mark. Many pioneers have paved the way for you. Continue to pave the way for future generations. If you don't identify as AAPI, you can still play a big role. Support AAPI communities. Amplify AAPI achievements. Everyone can promote racial justice. You can choose a better world.

Here are some activities to promote AAPI in STEM:

- Interview AAPI women working in a STEM field. Learn about what they do. Learn about their education and training. Learn about some of the obstacles they face. Write profiles about them. Send the profiles to your local newspapers. Help them get recognized.

- Host a STEM fair. Set up activities that will excite others about STEM. Encourage AAPI girls, including Southeast Asians and Pacific Islanders, to attend.

- Make a traditional Asian dish. Use math by measuring everything correctly. Use science to figure out how and why ingredients work together and how food changes when cooked. Make a cooking video and upload to YouTube. Include science and math facts as captions, as well as cultural and historical facts about the dish.

EXTEND YOUR LEARNING

Loh-Hagan, Virginia. *A is for Asian American: An Asian Pacific Islander Desi American Alphabet Book*. Ann Arbor, MI: Sleeping Bear Press, 2022.

Nichols, Hedreich, and Kelisa Wing. *Excellence in STEM*. Ann Arbor, MI: Cherry Lake Publishing, 2022.

Public Broadcasting Service: Asian Americans
https://www.pbs.org/weta/asian-americans

Reeves, Diane Lindsey. *STEM: Exploring Career Pathways*. Ann Arbor, MI: Cherry Lake Publishing, 2017.

GLOSSARY

actuaries (AK-chuh-wehr-eez) people who compile and analyze statistics and use them to calculate insurance risks

aerospace (EHR-oh-spays) branch of technology concerned with both aviation and space flight

AIDS (AYDZ) Acquired Immunodeficiency Syndrome; a disease in which the body can't fight infections

bored (BOHRD) made a hole in something

clone (KLOHN) to make identical copies of an organism's cells

cloud storage (KLOWD STOHR-ij) a way to store data on the internet

congress (KAHN-gruhs) formal meeting

doctorate (DAHK-tuh-ruht) the highest degree awarded by a university

explosives (ik-SPLOH-sivz) substances used to blow up something

HIV (AYTCH EYE VEE) Human Immunodeficiency Virus; the virus that causes AIDS

information superhighway (in-fuhr-MAY-shuhn soo-puhr-HI-way) electronic network such as the internet used for rapid transfer of information

material scientist (muh-TIHR-ee-uhl SYE-uhn-tist) person who studies the properties of solid materials

meteorologist (mee-tee-uh-RAH-luh-jist) person who studies weather and climate

microorganisms (my-kroh-OR-guh-nih-zuhmz) tiny organisms that can only be seen with a microscope

optical (ahp-TIH-kuhl) relating to light or the ability to see

pandemic (pan-DEH-mik) contagious illness that spreads worldwide

pensions (PEN-shuhnz) retirement funds for employees

respirator (reh-spuh-RAY-tuhr) mask worn over the mouth and nose to filter out dangerous substances

sexism (SEK-siz-uhm) unjust distinction based on gender

statistics (stuh-TIH-stiks) branch of mathematics dealing with the collection, analysis, interpretation, and presentation of masses of numerical data

structural engineering (STRUHK-chuh-ruhl en-juh-NIHR-ing) branch of civil engineering that deals with large modern buildings

tenured (TEN-yuhrd) having a permanent position

INDEX